DEAL OF FATES

(AN UNMAPPED JOURNEY)

ABISHEK.J

Made with ♥ on the Notion Press Platform
www.notionpress.com

Contents

Preface

"As I pencilled the words of "Deal of Fates" I couldn't help but reflect on the intricate web of destiny that binds us all. This story is a testament to the resilience of the human spirit, a reminder that even in the darkest moments, hope can be found. Join me on this journey into the lives of Ethi and Preethi, two souls entwined by fate".

Prologue

"Pause your imagination! for a while. Its nothing to deal with it.

Chennai's sweltering heat wrapped around the city like an living entity, its pulse beating in rhythm with the lives of its inhabitants. Amidst the cacophony of horns and chatter, two souls moved unknowingly toward each other, their fates entwined like the threads of a rich tapestry. Ethi whose life's bad luck spins out of control when he was kid and Preethi who had a streak of bad luck since she was a kid. These strangers bound by destiny were about to embark on a journey, whether that journey change their fate of lives ?"

Disclaimer

"All Characters, Organizations and events depicted in this novel, "Deal of fates" are entirely fictional and imaginary. Any resemblance to real individuals, living or deceased is purely coincidental.

This novel contains explicit content including Child Abuse, Violence, Strong language and Emotional distress. Reader discretion is advised. Suitable for readers 16+ only. The author and publisher do not endorse or promote harmful activities."

I

A New fate knocks Ethi's door

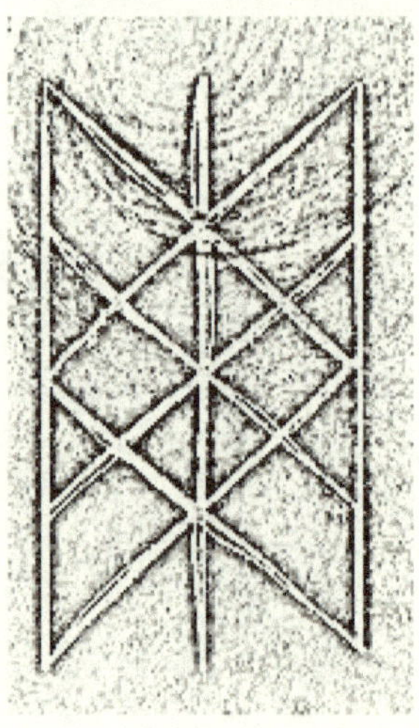

THE WEB OF WYRD

The local bar near the slum in Chennai was crowded with politicians from many parties. The inside bar was flooded with white shirts of politicians who came for that bar tender. It was noisy as splitting everyone's ears. There raised a voice in a mike announcing, "Selvam won the tender by a difference of fifty percentage points in votes". As soon as it was announced all the party members of him cheered, Woohoo! with a lot of whistling sound. By sitting in a chair, Selvam turned to them with a Proud laughter.

A few hours later, the Selvam gang sat for a drink. There was a sudden change of song from the radio; it started to play a rap song with a trumphet score and unknown lyrics. There Stepped the dirty torn shoes of the boy through the side entrance, whose hair was long and wild with a sharp end at the corner of his right eyebrow, walked along with the rap in a classy way by holding a herbal cigarette in the tip of his lips. He was in search of Selvam, later he found him and sat behind him.

Then Selvam ordered, "Turn off the shit, playing these kinds of songs with complicated lyrics and making everyone a hero." That boy called Selvam, "Anna, Anna," in a low tone since the crowd was noisy, he wasn't able to hear him. Then he called Selvam by touching his shoulder. Selvam turned towards him and saw him firmly, he noticed him inside and out; He was dressed in a faded orange shirt with a faded black pant and his face looked too young and creamy. All of the members in his gang asked him, "What you have come here for?" Then that boy replied with a normal tone, "I am Ethi; I came here to warn Selvam Anna." All the members over there laughed out of their bellies by his answer. One of the men asked Ethi in a sarcastic way, "Warning for what?, Not to knock the door of your mom's house at night", Ethi didn't get triggered for his question and replied with the same body language, "To quit from his recent post." Selvam controlled his laugh by hiding with a smile and asked him, "What if not?" Ethi replied with nervousness, "I'll make it done." Selvam said with a same smile, "See, your warnings are like kids reciting rhymes to a teacher; by your warnings, I should quit my post so that you can leave this place without any wound in your body." Selvam prepared his hands to hit him by rising from his place since he was too young to warn him. Ethi noticed this and unexpectedly hit his head with a whisky bottle near him, Ethi asked him with a carefreely, "Is it enough for you to quit Anna?".

Then suddenly all of his gang members aroused from their seats and started to choke Ethi's neck and push him to the next table. Ethi was jammed by six men, he can't even have space for his breath, and he started to lift the table from down, all the men rolled to the opposite floor. Selvam rised from the floor and noticed his head was drained of blood due to excessive bleeding; He choked Ethi and punched his face simultaneously. Ethi blocked him and pushed him narrowly towards the wall and all his members caught Ethi's hands firmly. Selvam, "You half-baked little thug, gonna fry you entirely." Selvam took a big nail from the broken table and ran towards Ethi, he cleverly used his legs to kick Selvam, and he fell on the chair, the chair got broken; hence, he was a large man.

Then Ethi's hands were still locked firmly by his gang, and suddenly the inspector of that street came with cops, knowing the information. He separated them, and he saw Ethi, where he noticed him; he didn't find any similarities with the politicians over there so, he suspected him. He slapped him. Ethi felt hesitated and lost his confidence by overcoming that; he slapped the inspector back. All the drunkards over there got shocked. Ethi felt something not yet finished for what he came for, so he ended up with this. He was arrested with his boss Santa and the cops beat them black and blue; Santa had no influence to tackle this.

The next morning dawned, and in another part of the city, Faisol, who was the son of AI Company owner Ammar, was restless by seeing his phone in his room as he was waiting for his PA Vincent's call. Faisol sent him to a particular hospital to seek a person for his illegal work, which was to abort the woman's pregnancy without her knowledge, who was none other than his girlfriend.

Meanwhile in the station, Selvam came with his minister to release his party members, who were all arrested along with Ethi and Santa, and he released them. Ethi felt some inferior over him that his boss had no influence. While Selvam talking to the inspector about the last-night incident, the minister was standing near the cell of Ethi and Santa. Santa asked him, "Sir, please! release us, we can also work for you." The minister replied arrogantly, "What can you do more than sitting useless like this behind bars?, The guy who sent you may be a fool like you guys; don't know whom to believe for his job, I also don't know, how he was fit into politics." Santa replied, "If it comes to politics race, we need to believe everyone blindly for bringing down the opponent, it's just a role of one's ego." The minister replied haughtily, "Guys like you should be behind bars; that's safe for the politics," and he left from there. Santa said to Ethi sarcastically, "It seems like these guys are outside the bars to protect the nation," with a laugh.

Later that day, Faisol lost his patience and rang his PA to ask whether the job was done. Vincent took his call; his face widened with lots of disappointments and he replied, "Man! No ladies over here were not ready to do it, hence this hospital was run by Christians all seems so spiritual, and even the ladies working here as sweepers denied it by saying, it's a curse, and they fear God." Faisol got erupted and replied, "You bastard, don't blabber anything in the name of helping me;

settle them money to shut their mouth." Vincent replied, "I did it so already," with the same disappointment. Faisol felt a deep relief and asked him calmly, "Ok! where you are now?" Vincent figured out his surroundings and replied, "Now I am just far away from her regular check-up hospital, and this place seems like a slum." Faisol felt satisfied and replied him, "What slum? Ok Vincent now, listen to me clearly, what we going to do was an illegal one and everyone knows about it, so we want a guy who was chill out to do anything without thinking its good or bad, so as our plan was sensitive it won't work with adults instead go for teen guys who loves to do anything for a fame or money as you said slum the job become easier for you and me, so choose a guy and call me back" and he cuts the call. Vincent wiped his eyes by removing the specs and remaind confused for his next move.

Later, in the same slum there was a Party meeting, the leader of the party member want some persons to arrange the meeting like placing chair, arranging the stage since he lost many party members for the past years. He requested some group of boys to do that who were opposite gang to Ethi and they replied, "We won't work for useless party like you." He stared them firmly and they moved from there with laughter. He encourages some kids to do that and they too denied that offer. One Locality man arrived by noticing this and said to him, "These kids only work for their godfather Santa because he helped them in parents meeting by acting as their dad, punishing the teachers who punished them and buying ice creams for them weekly once". The party leader asked them, "If I buy ice creams for you, will you work for me?" with a smile. The kids said, "It's enough for us to chant for your speech, please! Find our Santa to work for you" and they laughed. The locality man informed him, "That guy was arrested last night, he was not even worth and he was very silly man" The party leader replied, "These guys who don't even have their voter identities are very well known about politics, one who trained them must be a politics minded fellow, let me meet him." As that party leader has support among women in that slum and Santa was just a suspect the inspector released him. The Inspector said, "Take him alone with you, and leave this kid he needs to learn about basic discipline." Santa too left him and got released, Ethi felt betrayed. Then the Inspector asked Ethi, "In which beliefs you are dare to slap me? Even your well known man left you in the middle. Ethi remained calm for his questions inside the cell.

On the other side, Vincent was roaming near the hospital streets. There he met his brotherly friend outside of the Police station, he was none other than the same Inspector who came to bar and arrested Ethi. He called his brotherly friend inside the station and gave him some refreshments. Vincent noticed the station was very calm and there were no culprits except Ethi. Then he asked his friend, "What brother this station seems like an ancient museum, whether this street was free of crimes? there were not even a Pickpockets." The Inspector by mocking Ethi replied, "Even the Pickpockets are safe in their work, only guys like him are silly and childish in their work and make our duty easy." And they both laughed at him, Ethi remained silent again.

Then Vincent decided to leave from that station, he thanked his brother for sharing time with him. He rose from his seat and yet to move, as soon as he moved The Inspector said, "You know what he did? He even slapped me last night, annoying pest." Vincent was froozen for a moment of second, stood over there, turned his head slowly to him and left that place.

Vincent rang Faisol immediately and Faisol too attended his call in a first ring. Faisol was wondered and asked, "What Vincent? whether the job was done?" He replied calmly, "Yes! Sir",. Faisol asked, "Really! who was that?", Vincent turned his face to that station once again and replied, "A teen guy, age around eighteen or nineteen, seems like he was fearless to do anything without minding the situations and persons in front of him. Faisol with a satisfaction replied to him, "Then settle him money and own him soon." Vincent saw the station again and replied, "But he was in the locker man, seems like he was the only culprit in station." Faisol murmured, "Okay, man we will own him, I'll arrange for his release."

Then Faisol arranged some advocates to release him and it was done so.

After his release, the inspector warned Ethi, "Don't do these kind of silly things again which makes our duty easier and especially dont try to pretend like these guys in the notice board and you are not even near to them" by pointing out the wanted notice board in the station. And the Inspector crossed the road from the station to take his car, while Vincent thanking the advocates. Ethi plagued by doubts and asked Vincent, "Sir! you?" Vincent replied, "Hey! you, I am Vincent,are you happy now?"with lots of smile in his face. Ethi replied, "Yes! sir, but who are you?, what for you released me?" Vincent put his hand over his shoulders and said, "Nothing more, just a small job to be done by you." Ethi, "Ok! Tell me whats that?"

Vincent told him to wait in his place, then he took five lakhs from the bag which was inside the car. Vincent, "Keep it as advance is only for you" in a murmured tone and gave him a brand new cell phone with an inserted sim in a cover. Vincet smiled at him and said, "I contact you soon, now go home take some rest." Ethi remained doubtful till now and Vincent took his car, moved from there.

Moreover, the inspector opened his car door, stared Ethi who was in the opposite road; Ethi looked at the inspector back, The Inspector, "Stupid! useless bastard" and took his car. Ethi felt deeper insult in his heart, he got a mind disturbed. All the insults he faced since last night was running into his mind. And he felt he should do something big in front of everyone. He felt the need of having a proud attention from everyone in his streets especially The Inspector and the other cops.

He came back to his street; a teen boy around thirteen years came near to him and tried to shake his hands. And he said, "Wow! Brother, I know the news about yesterday, you just rocked all the cops and politicians by slapping the inspector " in a sarcastic tone. Unexpectedly he threw the ballon of water in his face and he ran away to the group of boys who was opposite gang to Ethi. They bullied him by saying, "See our street dog which roamed here and there become police dog now sorry! The Inspector dog, ha! ha! ha!" and they laughed harder. And Aryan a guy who always a disturbance for Ethi, asked him, "How do you got promoted as police dog in one night?", Ethi wiped the water from his face and replied, "You don't deserve the answer from me and a street bitich dog like you never deserve , don't repeat this silly things using silly boys." Aryan with a bashing tone shouted, "You motherfucker! let's see who's bitchy in this street" and they both started to fight each other. Ethi was in trouble because he can't handle his whole gang, suddenly Santa noticed this and helped Ethi, all the gang boys of him ran away. Then Santa and Ethi chased through crowded people and weaved some localities, finally caught them at the place of that Party meeting and both gang started to fought again by collapsing the arrangements of the chairs and stages.

Then The Party leader arrived and got shocked by seeing that. The locality man reminded him, "As I already said..." The

Party leader stared at him annoyingly. He then asked Santa, "Do you want to go to the locker again?" in a threatening way. Santa replied innocently, "Not me, only these kids did this." The Pary leader mocked at them and said, "You are the one said we won't work for useless party like you right? Run away from here", they replied arrogantly, "Why? Why we need to go?" and Aryan reminded him, "This is our street." Then the party leader said, "Ok! Let it be your street, but you should pay for this by seeking attention from your locality for my speech, there were no one ready to listen me even if I arrange this again, so say me the way to seek them." Santa gang suggested him, "If our boss sings, entire slum will gather here." Suddenly the bully gang replied in chorus, "Ahw! we are not ready for the shitty voice." And they fought again; The Party leader warned them to be quiet.

The Party Leader called Santa and requested him, "Santa, sing for me; can you sing about your slum and our party?" Santa blushed with a smile by showing his teeth and felt nervous about taking the microphone. All the members of his gang cheered, "Santa, come on, get the microphone." Finally, Santa got the microphone and started to sing the song about his slum and his party in the Ganna style; some boys started to beat out the music on the old plastic water drums in their slum; all started to dance, even the Aryan's gang. Ethi was not in that mood; his mind always reminded him to see that cover, which contained a new phone. The slum was filled with dances, musics, ganna songs, and it evoked a blissful mood.

After Santa finished singing, the party leader, after exhausting himself, asked him, "What man your boys said, if you sing, the entire slum will gather here, but everyone is scolding us like we are drunkards?" Then Santa asked for an other chance and got the microphone, and he announced, "Ratchasan Party, providing 100 rupees of cash, one who gathers here." and he ran away by giving the microphone to him. The Ratchasan Party leader got shocked by his announcement.

Later that night, after all the dances, songs, and music were over, Ethi entered his room, unbuttoned his shirts for relaxation as he was so tired, and sat on his unclean bed. All of a sudden, that brand new phone rang with an incoming call. Ethi saw that from his bed and roused slowly from his bed, moved towards the phone. Ethi's face and mind were so nervous; slowly he moved his right hand to the phone and attended the call by pressing the green button.

There Vincent told their plan to Ethi and the way of doing that; he listened calmly.

Though he felt strange over his plans, he remembered all the insults he had faced since last night, to break that he was ready to accept the deal.

Vincent declared, "If this was done, the reward for you is 50 lakhs," in a strange tone.

Ethi fearlessly replied, "I'll do it double great for you, sir.".

With a new dawn, Kundhavali, a 48-year-old woman with a rounded figure, entered the Christian trust hospital, which was at the entrance of the slum. As soon as she entered, she visited the receptionist to clarify that her client was in the same room. And the receptionist clarified to her that she was in the same room. She opened her client room. She saw her client was looking outside the window by sitting on her bed, drapped in a rosewood-coloured saree. In her 8th month of her pregnancy, her face resembled like she had faced all the twists and turns of fate in her life; her thick black hair blazed, swept by the morning wind, and it gently brushed her shiny face, which all helped her to hide her pain over her face.

Kundhavali called her, "Preethi!, what are you thinking about?", Preethi changed her position of sitting and turned her head towards her with a smile, which holed a dimple in her face, and asked, "Nothing! Akka, when did you come?" Kundhavali replied, "Just now, dear, I brought your favorite badam milk; drink it soon as it was at fine temperature." Kundavali took all her fruits, tiffin boxes, and flasks from her wire basket and kept them on the near table. Then Kundhavali sat near Preethi and asked, "How many days are you going to take this pain alone? Where is he? Whether he knew you were pregnant?" She replied innocently, "Yes, Akka! He said there were some alliance torchers by his dad; he will be back soon." Kundhavali face widened with disappointments and said, "When? It's been almost seven months; now a days it's hard to believe boys from higher backgrounds." Preethi clamied suddenly, "No! akka, please! He was not like that; only after meeting him, I feel some change in my life. I need this change throughout my life; I believe he will grant me." Kundhavali, "Whatever Preethi, did you see all the other ladies in the hospital who came for a check-up with their man in their month of pregnancy? Doesn't that make you feel bad?" Preethi, with a cute smile, replied, "Why should I? If I have a caretaker like you" and hugged her. Kundhavali, with an emotional smile, touched her rosy, glossy cheeks and kissed her cheeks.

Later that same morning, Ethi got up from his bed, dressed in the same orange faded shirt and black faded pants, and saw the mirror to prepare himself. He took his sentimental knife for safety. He then fitted it between his belt like a cowboy. He left his house and went near the Christian trust hospital. As soon as he reached, his phone notified him of a message; he checked that, and he received her photo through MMS. There he saw her face, which was so innocent—a pure smile like a newborn baby. She has thick hair and a deep dimple on her face in that photo. Then he turned his head around, and his mind made him think that it was the toughest task, which was so emotional too. Ethi fixed his mind; there was no chance of turning back, and he moved on. He searched for her in windows to make his job easier. Later he found her; he saw her for the first time; she was drinking her badam milk, and he verified her face with that photo.

He then entered the hospital; he kept his cover, which was given by Vincent, that not alone contained a brand new phone, and he took one syringe, some unknown liquid substance, and some tablets; it's all to make the job without violence. Then he took one safety mask near the table, and he wore that.

Kundhavali left her room to go to the washroom. He then entered Preethi's room; she was seeing the window with a thought of her boyfriend's arrival. Ethi inserted that unknown substance into the syringe; she noticed him, and she was blank by seeing that. She asked him, "Whether it's for me? The doctor prescribed me, no more injections until the delivery time come." Ethi said strongly, "But she informed me to inject as your delivery date was near." Preethi aroused from her bed and said, "I verify with her; you may be addressing the wrong person." Preethi was widened with doubts. Ethi, "She won't be available today, so she informed me; it's just a vaccination; no need to fear; show your arm quick." Then her caretaker entered the room and was shocked by Ethi's presence. Kundhavali asked, "Who are you?" Preethi all of a sudden replied for his question, "He came to vaccinate me, Akka." Her caretaker was shocked as hell and stated, "There were no male staff members working here." Suddenly a nurse opened the door and asked the same question to him, "Who are you?" in a doubtful manner by seeing the syringe in his hand and a mask in his face.

In the blink of an eye, Ethi took his knife, which was in-between his belt, and scratched her in the below neck, and she felt down on the floor. Preethi ran towards him, caught his hand tightly, and pushed the syringe out of his hands. Ethi slapped her to the wall. Forgetting the presence of her caretaker, he bent down to take the syringe, which was under the cot, and he noticed that needle was broken in the syringe. Her caretaker was shivering in fear as she was old; she silently moved towards the half-opened door to call someone. Ethi noticed her, dragged her leg from down, and she fell on the floor, and she screamed, "Ahw!". Preethi was yet to call somebody. He then quickly got up and closed her mouth, pushed her towards the wall. She was seeing him eye to eye; her eyes were filled with tears and innocence, and she started to punch him on the stomach using her right hand.

Ethi suddenly took his knife from his pants; while taking the knife, it hurt her right hand fingers, so she stopped punching him. Then he turned his head to the right side to avoid her eye contact. Ethi's eyes were filled with stubborn tears. He closed her mouth tightly and pointed out her stomach for an attack. While he started to attack, she placed her left hand in front of her stomach for blocking and injured her palm and five fingers. He continued that for six times, rapidly using a knife by closing his eyes, her blood splattered over his face. Then he stopped by a deep breath, and she slowly slid down from the wall. He then ran away through the half-opened doors. Lastly, she saw only his dirty, torn shoes as he ran away, and she laid down.

Ethi dragged Kundhavali from down and headed towards Preethi

II

TWIST OF FATES

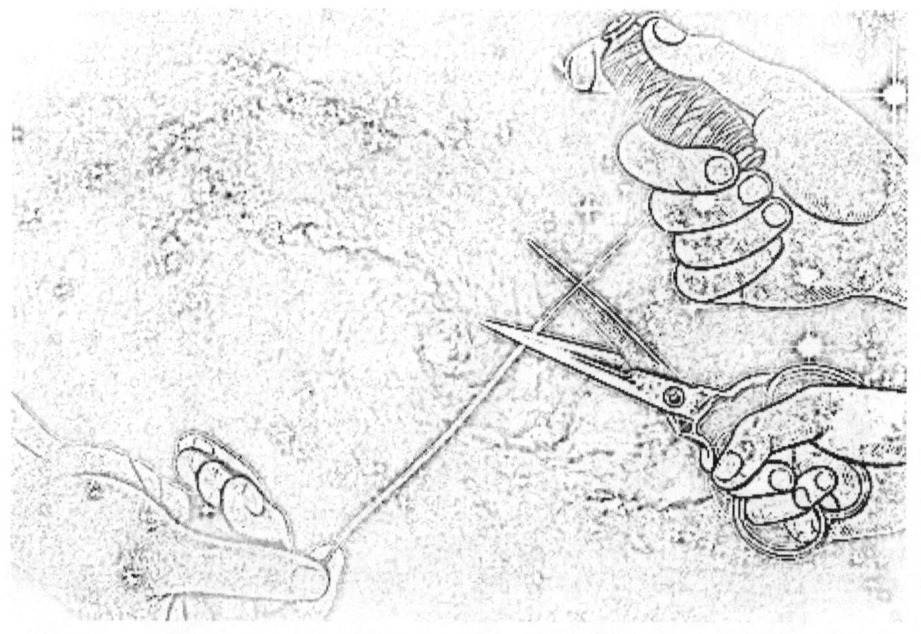

The Moirai

As the hours went by that night, Ethi entered the old well, which was used as a bar for partying, rarely for some relaxation. There his boss arranged a party to show off his thug. Ethi remaind unsuprised and went to the corner table. Then the bar dancer of their street joined their party; her striking features shone under the dim lights, her eyes sparkled with a hint of mischief, and her smile could light up the entire room. Her outfit was a dazzling display of color and texture, and her high heels accentuated her long legs. Then the dim bar pulsed with energy after her presence, which made Ethi to join the party with the music and drinks. Bottles of whiskey and rum were opened simultaneously by all men, their contents splashing over the outdoor top and spilling onto the men's shirts, pants, and hands. The air reeked of alcohol and sweat.

An Alcoholic Well

Suddenly, Ethi felt something strange over himself while dancing; he stopped dancing and went to the same corner table again for relaxation. Santa called him, "Ethi, come on, my man, you become a star overnight; I know everything;

come let's cheer," Ethi asked in a strange tone, "Where was the source for this party?" Santa replied, "From your advance," with lively, dirty dance movements. Ethi stared at him calmly, and Santa moved with a hesitated smile and continued his dirty steps.

A man in the corner misbehaved with that bar dancer by hugging her from her back. Ethi headed towards him as she belonged to his neighboring street, started to push him from her, and slammed him to the table. Then the man got up slowly by catching his back; the party got stopped, and he said, "You insulted me in the name of party Santa." He went away from that place, and all the men over there started to wind up.

ꙮ

ꙮ

Ethi came outside the well and sat on a stone; there came a man in the darkness. His eyes and his smile were scary in the darkness. He was at his 70, gaunt and bald with some long gray hairs at his back and more gray hairs near his cheeks and chin. He was dressed in a dirty checked shirt with an Indian lungi. He came closer to Ethi and sat near with him and said, "You need some philosophies of mine, manly child." Ethi took a herbal cigarette and said, "Take this and move away" in a rough tone. The old man stated, "Sorry! It's too late to convice me; your face seems like you are worrying for some of your victory." Ethi stared at him strangely. The old man said, "See my child, money and fame make many things; if one paisa or one victory makes you feel bad, just throw it away for whom it deserves." Ethi got frustrated and moved out from there. The old Philosopher blabbered, "You can't sleep tonight kid, throw the money away". Ethi went to his room, stared at his knife, and soon he laid down and slept silently.

The following morning, Ethi woke up earlier than usual; he was curious to see what was going on at the hospital. He saw the view of that hospital from his home; it was as usual. He expected some intimidation by cops, but there were not even the cars of cops. Ethi went back to the hospital; there also he found no one. The hospital was as usual, and it followed its regular routine. Ethi scratched his chin using his hand, and his eyes were full of mystry. He decided to move from the entrance of the hospital. While he was crossing, he heard a voice in a particular room's window. A mysterious expression widened across Ethi's face. He saw Preethi over there; she was sitting with her bandaged fingers on both hands. Ethi's mind confused him by giving mixed emotions over her. Ethi hidden his presence from her by leaning near the wall of the window. There her caretaker asked, "Why do you remind me to be silent while the cops introgate with you? Do you know who was that boy? Do you know him before? Why he wants to kill you, when you are in this stage?" Preethi remained silent for all her questions; later she answered, "I don't know who he was."? and I don't want to clarify anything about the incident, Akka." Kundhavali remained unsatisfied with her answer for a minute and asked her furiously, "Preethi, your answer didn't make any sense. Did you notice his words and actions? It was all about terminating your baby. Can't you be aware of that? Let me take you to the cops again or your fiance." Preethi said with frusturation, "I don't want to disturb him; he was already disturbed. I don't want to make any sensitive issue about me, and I was done with what happened yesterday!. Let anything can happen; I want my new life to get started with Faisol and with our baby."
The caretaker was disappointed, turned her roughly, and

asked her with some curiosity, "What made you to be dumb like this? If it was me or any other woman, we would make him count the bars behind the cell." Preethi face swelled up with sorrows, and she replied, "The things I had faced in my life, which contained trust issues, betrayal, and hardships, taught me this. Even the small things happened in my life weren't even predictable. In one usual word, I can explain to you, it's all my fate written from my birth." Kundhavali touched her glossy cheeks and said with a hopeful smile, "Dear, its common in everyone's life; you seem too young. How do you experience these many things at this age?" Preethi said with painful laughter, "This age? It all started when I missed my mom." Kundhavali, "Are you blaming your dad? or someone in your relation?" Preethi turned from her face and replied, "I don't know whom to blame, Akka."

Preethi wiped her tears over his eyes and opened up to her

Preethi, "My dad was a retired army man. When I was 8, my mom had passed away. Rumours around my surroundings believed; my dad always tochered my mom in the name of sex, and he even raped her many times. And because of those struggles, she ended her life by hanging. These rumors made my school staff members and students keep a distance from me. This made me get attached more to my father. He used to bathe me and take care of all my physical needs in the place of mom. The rumors about my father became true day by day after I reached my teen age. The day which I can still remember, and even the time it was around 12 o'clock, I was sleeping in my bed since I had a heavy fever. My dad was having his regular drinks by watching television. While I was sleeping, I found someone raising my skirt and tried to touch my bottom. I aroused from my bed with drowsy eyes, and I noticed my father was standing in front of me. His body was nervous, and he stated, "I checked whether you have pads or not since you

were sleeping; I cannot ask you. Okay! I think I disturbed your sleep; take this tablet with you for better sleep," and he smiled. My room was totally dark, and I couldn't see the tablet, he was giving me. I had no mindset to doubt him, as he was father to me. I took the tablet and I laid down. I felt some changes in my mood after some minutes. He suddenly laid back on me and raised my skirt again to touch my thighs and bottom. Even then, I had no doubt over his touches.

The next day I got ready for school. I took my bicycle, and I started to pedal. While pedaling for a few meters, I felt down accidently from my bicycle. My father took me back home and said, "Okay! Let's take leave for today since you injured your knee heavily." He took me to the restroom to apply some ointment to my knee. He took that and poured that in a cotton. I raised my uniform skirt for my first aid. He asked me to raise a little further, and I did it just above my knee. He asked for again, and I raised a little bit. He got frustrated and ordered me with a based tone, "Lift up like this," and he raised my skirt to the top all of a sudden. I jerked away his hands and moved back from him. He then changed his face to normal and said, "Dear, did I trouble you more? It's only for your safety purposes, or else you would get more bleeding." While requesting to me, he slipped down in front of the washroom floor. I realized the rumors were true, and my head started to shiver. He was trying to get up from the floor, and while he got up, he stared at my leg from down. I can see his real intention on his face; it was full of lust. He touched my skirt, and as soon as he touched it, I took his empty beer bottle and hit on his head. He felt down with full of blood, and I took my school bag to run away from him. He crawled to stop me by calling me, "Preethi! Preethi!

Only at the age of 16, I know all his intentions are to get me. I also realized his touches were all wrong even when I was a kid. At the age, I don't know to whom I should say this, and I can't come out of this till now. After him, money became my biggest enemy until I met Faisol. I work as well as I study for my school fees. I don't know whether it's God's grace or my fate has gone after that I got college for less fees with a free hostel. See who will think about getting his daughter in bed using tablets. By comparing this, the incident what happened yesterday does not seem to be a big fate to me as my good days are near. " The caretaker exhibited a heart full of sympathy for Preethi with care and asked, "What if he comes again to take your life?" Preethi remained calm; her eyes started to flood up with tears, and she answered with a pittyful tone.

"I cry, I cry, I beg, I beg for my new life and beg him by saying, I should be there at least for my baby."

All these were heard by Ethi with a struggling emotion; he fought back his tears by wiping that all over his face.

III

Deal her fate

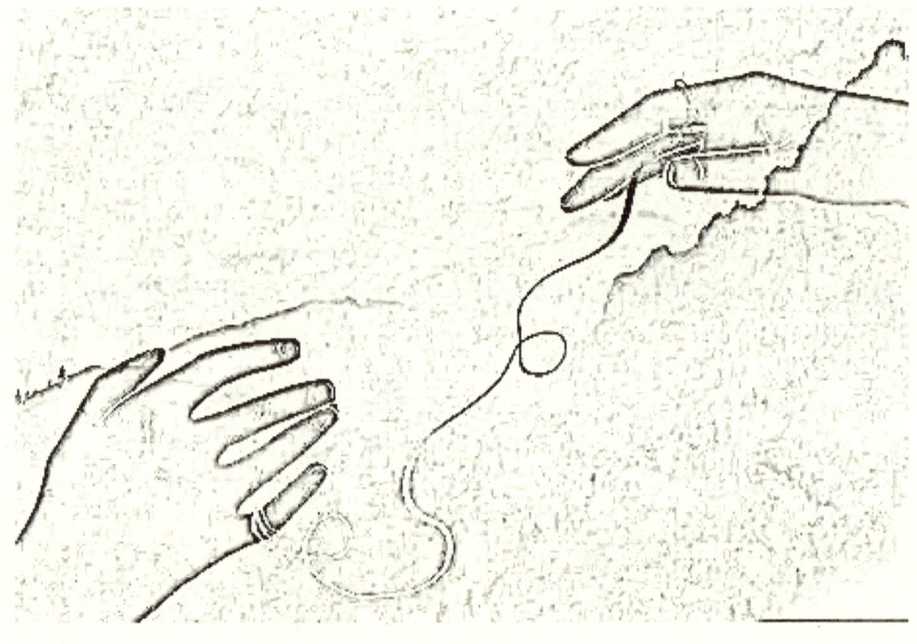

The Red thread of fate

Then Ethi went into the hospital; he saw the receptionist; he went near her; he saw a bunch of cards that contained motivational lines; he took a card from that; it had printed lines of, "You've survived the darkest nights; the dawn of you was so near." He asked the receptionist, "Is it free of charge?" as she was a muted woman and couldn't reply by words. She shook her right finger with a smile and gestured "No!". Then Ethi took from his pants pocket 50 rupees without asking for its cost, and she handed him that card by refusing his money with a smile. He looked confused; his face resembled oily from the moisture as he had shed tears a moment before. Then she took a donation box from that hospital and gestured to that box, indicating he should put his money inside. Ethi smiled by looking at that box and put his money inside. Then he handed her the card back and pointed to Preethi's room from where he was and gestured for her to give that card to her. She showed a thumbs up with an energitic smile and headed towards her room.

The muted receptionist opened the door of her room. Kundhavali saw her with a smile, and she was about to move towards the half-open door. Within a millisecond, the opposite vacant room was consumed by a massive bomb blast. The exploded bricks from the room hit the muted woman head with an incredible force, faster than lightning. Kundhavali was thrown against the wall by the force of a blast. Some exploded bricks shattered against Preethi's head, which drove her to semi-consciousness. A group of boys, hurrying to beat the clock, arrived from far opposite to Ethi. With haste, they tossed a smoke grenade inside Preethi's room to make her completely unconscious. All patients and people over there ran against the time towards the entrance to save their lives. The floor was scattered with smoke of grenades. Ethi froozed at the same place. By noticing all this, he started to move by seeing the face covered with a kerchief, which was similar to him. As he was moving, suddenly a brave security dashed him from his back and went towards them. With a fraction of a second, a boy emerged from smoke and jumped towards Ethi; he was with a sharp black blade. Ethi moved from him, hence he was targeting him; unfortunately, he targeted the security who was near Ethi's shoulder and forcefully inserted his blade into his neck. The blood was spilled from his neck to his toes, and he fell down. Ethi's eyes were remained blank by his move, and he saw the boy eye to eye. He stared at him firmly and moved back towards his gang. There Ethi saw a boy who had the scar on his eyebrow in that gang, and then he realized it was Aryan. Aryan, by mocking Ethi, warned him, "Hey! Inspector dog, what are you doing on here? This is our new task; it seems you didn't complete the task; just leave away from here along with people, or you too will be aborted with the baby." And Aryan reminded his boys, "Listen all, we have only a short amount of time for our task; get it done faster until the squad arrives."

Ethi stayed silent, realized it was none of his business, and stepped backward with his foot and head towards the entrance. Ethi turned his head towards the glass in the reception area, his red, tear-filled eyes. The glass reflected multiple faces of him, but all revealed the same truth: he had become a senseless, stonehearted monster because of the thirst he had for money and fame.

Then Aryan and his boys are ready for their task. A boy over there inserted an unknown liquid substance into the syringe, and he headed towards her room. An unknown hand of someone emerged from the smoke, grabbed his collar from behind, and slammed him to the floor. Then his wild hair sprang up from the darkness, his red eyes glowing through smoke like a crocodile's, patiently waiting for its prey in a dark sea; his face emerged ferociously from the smoke; then he

rose up fearlessly and stomped on the syringe needle. Aryan noticed that it was Ethi.
Then the old fire alarm echoed through the air as he moved towards them. Every head turned towards the sound; the warning was clear: the fire was near.

Ethi tightened his fist, which brought out his nerves. The smoke began to clear slowly. Ethi can clearly see their eyes in covered faces and their street weapons gripped tightly in their hands. Aryan bashed out and said, "Hey! Why are you staring at him? Just throw him off; we are running out of time." As soon as he ordered, all started to ran towards him. Ethi sprang into action, rolling towards the first boy who came near him and pierced his foot by taking the needle of a broken syringe. All the boys covered over him; Aryan took advantage of that and prepared a boy for going inside her room with a syringe. Ethi cleverly picked up a stretcher from his near room and blocked all of them using that, and he narrowly rolled on the structure through the inbetween spaces. Aryan urged his guy to go inside; he stepped to her room as soon as he stepped. Ethi choked his neck from the back using his arms, lifted his arms, took that syringe from his hand, and pierced it forcefully to his above chest. Aryan attacked Ethi's knee from his back using an iron rod and choked his neck with that. Ethi severely injured in his knee, Aryan threw a new syringe to a boy and said, "Go! Quick, I take care of him" in a hurried manner. Ethi moved his hands to the back and took an exploded brick and used that to hit Aryan's head; it broke into two pieces. He took another piece of brick, targeted the boy head who was inside, and quickly tossed the brick to his head. He jerked down to the floor.

Then Ethi dragged his bad knee towards Preethi's room; he put all his body to shield her; he was at the entrance of her room; he breathed heavily by seeing them. Four boys covered him with knives and blades. Unexpectedly, a boy scratched his bad knee using a knife, and Aryan hit his head using an iron rod. Ethi vision was blurred; he saw Preethi through his blurred vision that she moaned heavily even in her unconscious state. Aryan silently moved in the side. Surprisingly, Ethi took his sentimental knife from his pant and aggressively pierced in the exploded wall to block him. All got panicked by his sharp knife and moved a little back; in the blink of an eye, he scratched a boy like a wild cat who was ahead of him in his underneck. All the boys of him left Aryan in the middle, and they ran away.

Aryan threatened him using a blade and pushed his knife out of his hand by scratching his hand using a blade. Ethi was semi-unconscious for a while. Aryan took advantage, and he was about to raise a heavy attack on him. At lightning speed, Ethi choked his neck, slammed him on the stretcher, and attacked his shoulder harsly using his own blade six times. Aryan's blood splattered over his face, and in his orange shirt, with a bloody face, Ethi looked like a battered hunting dog.

Later, he locked Aryan in one room with the stretcher; he dragged his bad Knee to Preethi's room. He noticed her; she was inactive, and there were no actions in her. Ethi dragged his bad knee and moved towards her with a racing pulse in his hands. He checked her by raising the hands and slapping her cheeks, and he hesitated to place his ear on her breast to check whether she was alive or not. He noticed her bed; it was pouring with blood. He saw that there was bleeding from her vagina. Ethi was in some hope that she might be alive. He saw that it started to pour again. Ethi breathed heavily by figuring out the atmosphere for the next move. He dragged his bad knee to the reception and saw the notice board displaying a list of a few doctors names and their contact information. He tried them using the hospital landline; some of them were busy and some of them were unreachable. He tried one doctor contact, and suddenly he heard a sound of the ring. It made him sweat from head to toe, and the droplets of his sweat mixed with his blood and dropped down like water from an unopened tap. Sadly, the call was denied. Ethi dropped his hands on the table, blurred for a while, and breathed heavily simultaneously. Ethi dragged his bad knee back to her room; he noticed that pouring never stops. He then moved towards the exploded window and noticed a little hostage of slum people through the exploded window who were a little far away from the hospital. He made his way out through the exploded window to seek their help. He put all over his body to reach them. Finally he came near to them; all started to step back their foot by his blood-shattered appearance, soaked in his face and in shirts. Ethi accidently fell down on the broken fence and exhibited his pain by closing his eyes. He got up badly from the ground of sand. All stepped a little back again. Ethi pointed out the hospital and requested, "A girl in the hospital was bleeding" in a tensed manner. Ethi doesn't know how to explain the situation to them, as he was too little to handle. The people over there felt scared at his face and chased him away. Then he noticed an old lady over there and started to request her, "Patti, please! Come over there; I promise you this situation won't harm you." The old lady remained silent and moved back towards the people; suddenly Preethi moaned heavily in labor pain, which reached to the ears of the people.

Then the old lady started to run towards the hospital after hearing her moanings. She entered the hospital and rubbed her palm, shielding her head by using her saree from sunlight. By noticing Ethi's nervous feet, she reminded him, "She's alive, son, relax, and why can't you say there she's pregnant? Poor child, only God saved her." By seeing her closed eyes, Ethi remained hesitated. She reminded him, "Please! Call the doctor; I was not in touch for more than a year and lack experience in supporting women during delivery; look at her bed; it seems more critical." Ethi face widened with disappointments and replied, "There was no one who took the call, Patti." Ethi went to the reception and tried for the same number, but she denied his call continuously.

Meanwhile, across the city, a lady doctor of that trust saw the founder of that hospital in road, and invited him to the car. He noticed her phone was continuing to receive calls. He stared at her phone and asked her, "Why are you rejecting these calls? It seems like from our hospital landline, is there any emergency case?" She replied casually, "Probably sir, but all patients wind up from the hospital after the bomb blast in a room, and I was very scared to go there until the squad arrives." The Founder erupted in anger, exclaiming, "Stupid! What if someone over there is in trouble, and that person is a patient?, you're disgrace to the medical field." She replied hesitatedly, "Seems everything was clear, sir; no patients were there." Founder didn't mind her words and ordered her driver to go to his hospital.

On the other side, Ethi was totally exhausted after trying the calls, and he looked out at the old lady with the frusturation. Then the old lady's eyes filled with tears, and by seeing the top, pressing her palms, she prayed to her god silently. There the founder and the lady doctor rushed into the hospital with some nurses. The founder stared at Ethi firmly since his face was familiar to him. There the nurses ordered Ethi to stay out of her room. Ethi silently moved with regret. The old lady helped them by holding Preethi's hand tightly. The lady doctor ordered the nurses to clean her pubic area since it was bleeding. She was tensed because Preethi lost so much blood as per her view, when she saw the baby on the monitor; it was safe, not as much as they thought, and they delivered her baby safely by the method of vaginal delivery. The infant uttered his first words to his new world in loud cries.

Ethi had a deep breath, and the old lady thanked God by exclaming, "Murugaaa...!". The founder appreciated her; after delivery, he noticed that it was a boy and warned her not to repeat this mistake again. Later, the founder saw Ethi; he analyzed it was very familiar face to him and stated, "The worst fate was she believed a boy like you; take care of her baby as a good husband" by misunderstanding them as a couple. The lady doctor informed the founder that Preethi will be unconscious for some days as she lost excessive blood.

The Founder handed over the new born baby to Ethi

The Founder handed over the boy child to Ethi, he got that baby with shivering hands and he took the boy child to his home.

IV

Fate joins Fate

The Wheel of Dharma

Later that night, Ethi saw her baby firmly, which was in his dirty bed, layered with a white towel from the hospital.

Suddenly, the little one started crying by closing his eyes. Ethi rose up from his floor and took him. He can't bear his sounds; he saw outside of his window that the moonlight was clear and his slum was so dark. He wrapped the little one using his black shirt, quickly opened the door, and he figured out his slum presence. He saw the closed doors of the slum, and the dog's long, mournful howl echoed in darkness. He headed towards the hospital for some help, and he found out it was under the investigation of Chennai cops. He turned back, realizing that it was not possible to go inside even without the baby; hence, he had already feud with the inspector. He saw the opposite slum residents gathered, barbecuing chickens and chatting with one another. He stepped softly towards them to hide his existence; the air was heavy with cold, and shadows danced on the walls. Then, without warning, an unknown hand pulled Ethi near the broken statue of the freedom fighter. Ethi got a moment of jerk and pushed the hands, and it jingled with a soft sound of bangles. There stood the bar dancer, Leela, a slim sparrow dressed with her same dazzling dress and high heels. She loved the jerked breath of Ethi towards her face. Ethi was dumb by seeing her; she saw him with her mischievous look. By holding his shirt firmly, she asked him, "Hey little thug, why are you roaming here? Did you come here to see, your Leela was safe, or do you want something which is beneficial for you and me? anything for this little thug" in an erotic tone. Ethi saw those people at her back who were a little far away. Leela, "Oh! My little thug feels so shy to take this Leela, so sorry! Show me your home from here or come to my sweet home" by pulling his shirt, and her palm accidentally touched his below abdomen, where she felt some huge thing.

Leela, in a confused state, asked Ethi, "What's wrong with your stomach?" and she touched that, and she saw a beautiful little face that was glowing in the moonlight. Leela's sharp eyes saw that child firmly. Leela, "What for you came here? Your face resembles guilt, but its not to bed a woman." Ethi looked around for a while and requested her, "Yes! I want something from you. I am sure you're aware of the bomb blast of the hospital in my slum. There I took him, and it seems his mother was no more. He's crying in hunger, and I can't bear it. Can you help him by your slum members? I cannot request them, since they know I have been involved in many child kidnaps." Leela was totally dumb where the nocturnal insects were chirping around them.

Leela walked from him, holding the child with shivering hands. There the old lady stopped her with a thin stick. She noticed Ethi near the broken statue. Ethi saw her face, which was familiar to him since he saw her in the morning. The old lady gestured for him by her hands to come out of the darkness. Later, she noticed it was him by the white bandage in his bad knee, which resembled a clear view to her in the night. She got the baby from Leela; she can read him for what he came for and gestured for him to wait there for a while. The old lady gave the little one to another mom in his slum for feeding him. She clarified the doubts of people by saying the child was an orphan since the bomb blast at the hospital in the morning. The people over there made him to sleep by singing some Tamil lullabies. The little one slept by closing his tiny fingers firmly.

Later, Leela arrived with the child and handed it over to Ethi. Leela, "He slept; don't disturb him and go to your home safely; don't worry, all are clear in my place; you can handover him to me anytime when he feels hungry." Ethi saw her face with relief, and he stepped back to wind up from there. Leela, "Take care, little hero, goodnight!" by gesturing her bangled hands as bye. A heartfelt smile spread across Ethi's face, thanking her silently.

A new day broke. Ethi was brushing his teeth outside; the little one was still sleeping near the window. As Ethi gargled his mouth with water, a thick tail suddenly crawled through the window. It lifted its head and headed towards the baby. Ethi heard a faint rustling sound of a reptile, opened the door, and his eyes chilled at the sight of a king cobra, mere inches from the baby. Ethi stepped slowly towards his sentimental knife; with the knife in his hand, he was trying to chase that away, but the cobra swiftly jerked his head, its eyes blazing with fury, poised to strike. He stepped back, grabbing his lighter from the table, and fired a cloth, using the flaming cloth to chase the cobra. But the snake evaded his attack with lightning speed, jerking its head backwards just inches from the flames. Ethi's heart skipped a beat as he watched in terror; the flames from the cloth dropped precariously towards the baby's bed, mere inches from the innocent child's face. He put the flaming cloth down, grabbed his sentimental knife, and heated its blade until the tip glowed fiery red. With a swift motion, he waved that towards the cobra's head, its body jerking backward as it sensed the intense heat, and it crawled back quickly towards the window, seeking escape.

Suddenly, the little one started it's cry, and with a swift motion, Ethi closed the door to prevent the attention from his localities. He ripped out a handful of cotton from his dirty bed and rolled it between his palms until it formed a fluffy sphere ball. He gave that to the infant to play; suddenly it stopped crying, rolled its eyes, looked firmly towards the fluffy ball, and started crying again. Ethi was dumb and sat down with a heavy breath on the floor.

As the days passed by, he devoted himself to caring for the little one every day. Each day brought a new routine: bathing him using warm clothes, dressing him, and feeding him, thanks to the kindness of other mothers. Ethi noticed every night that the cops were always investigating the wrong person for the past four days.

One fine morning, several days later in the hospital, Preethi eyes opened slowly with a fresh breath, and she awoke quickly by seeing her stomach; it was surprising flat and firm. The sudden realization hit her like a tidal wave: she had given birth. She was shocked as hell. The old lady entered her room with fruits and asked her, "Are you alright? You are lucky to have a husband like him, dear; you had a very safe delivery because of him." Preethi was shocked again and asked her, "What husband?" The old lady replied, "Yes! Doesn't he come to meet you?" Preethi remained calm for her questions and moved to the reception and asked about her delivery. The woman over there told her that it was handed over to her husband since she was in an unconscious state. She asked for his address; the receptionist got frozen for a while and gave her the address with a sarcastic smile.

Finally, Preethi got his address; she was in a confused state about If it were her fiance, why would he ghost her by taking her baby alone, and why he should stay in this local area. She decided to go to the particular address to clarify her doubts. At last she reached his home. She opened the door where she saw a boy from his backside who was preparing cerelac for her infant, and she also noticed the same orange shirt and the same knife on the table, which reminded her of that terrible day. She silently stepped towards the iron rod near the door, grabbed it firmly with her pale hands, and hit on his head. She expelled a glob of saliva onto his face and said, "You'd better off begging in the streets than putting a price on human life." She took her baby from his dirty bed and saw her baby for the first time with tears over her eyes. She quickly stepped backward to leave his house and went back to her hospital for her discharge.

When she was packing her stuff, the old lady asked her, "Where is your husband? Are you leaving alone?" Preethi raised her voice and stated, "The man whom you are mentioning was not my husband." The old lady remained calm, stopping her departure and reminded her, "But he was the one who saved you on your delivery by calling me and the doctor of you; you were unconscious at that time, dear." Preeth's face spread with a lot of confusion and she questioned herself, "He was the one who came to attack me; why should he save me again and whom he was to me?"

With a lot of questions in her mind, she returned to Ethi's home. There she saw Ethi's face clearly, which was too young for her. She asked him, "I don't know who you are; you seem too young to me. First of all, I am sorry, but please tell me why you want my baby? and who asked for it? I don't know who you're till now." Ethi told her to wait in her place, and he shut all the doors and windows and placed her a chair to sit. He sat opposite to her, and he couldn't tackle her eye contact; later, by overcoming that, he was about to explain her everything. Just as he began, a loud crash shook the door, splintering it open.

Santa and his burly goons burst in, storming towards Preethi and Ethi. Santa, with frusturation, asked Ethi, "If you can't do it properly, why can't you say to me its a huge offer for us?" Ethi hold the hands of Santa with a tense that contained a silver revolver and said, "No, lets deny this offer, as we people don't have anyone in life; she also likes the same, but this girl wants to live for her baby, and he was her only blood relation she has; lets leave her; I'll arrange some huge deal for you." Santa replied, "What, Ethi? You are talking so cinematic; I didn't come for the offer; I came here because her fiance threatened, if the job wasn't yet finished, he threatened he would prison us by the act of attempting murder on her girl friend as we blasted bombs on her; he misunderstood us, we attempted the job so violently and sensitively." Preethi was shocked to the core and asked Santa, "Did he really say that?"

Santa exclaimed, "Yes! Ahw, these kinds of boys."

Ethi was testing Santa's Emotion

Ethi kneeled down and tested Santa's emotion. Ethi declared, "I don't want to join in this cruel attempt anymore, and it gives me guilt after guilt, I give you two options Santa; deliver this girl and her baby to this address, or else take my life by your bullet and go on to your work." Preethi bent back of him with a lot of tears by holding her baby.

Santa loaded bullets in his rifle, pointed towards Ethi, and said, "I can't see your face anymore, Ethi; you are not the same Ethi anymore," and he turned his head back and triggered the rifle. He heard only the sounds of his riffle and avoided his eye contact since he had been with him for 10 years. Santa said, "Take his body out and poison her baby," and he turned his head back. He was surprised by the wild face of Ethi. Soon Santa realized Ethi didn't take his bullet, and Ethi realized Santa only wanted his task to be done rather than listening to his words.

In the blink of an eye, Ethi rose from his position and pointed his knife to Santa's side belly by turning his body and pointed the riffle on his forehead. Ethi said, "You didn't even change a bit, Santa; the fate is I should be with you," and he threatened Santa's goons by placing the knife and the rifle over their boss. He told Preethi to follow him. Santa warned, "Ethi, you're risking your life; there were also people outside who were all the goons of her fiance; please finish the task; it is good for you and me; they are here to check whether we did the job." Ethi remained calm and replied, "Oh! Is it?" and he shot two Chinese goons on their shoulders. Ethi told Preethi as well as Santa to enter into the car of the Chinese goons. He saw a man marching towards him with a Chinese blade. Ethi swiftly kicked a nearby flowerpot, sending it crashing to the ground. The attacker lost his footing, stumbling forward, seizing the opportunity, he shot on his arm while he was still mid-air. Ethi opened the door to get inside, and in the blink of an eye, Ethi got attacked by a knife in his elbow from his back by the goons. Preethi jerked back with her baby. Santa came out fearlessly to help Ethi, and they both battled with four of the guys, and Ethi counterattacked the goon by dashing him to the car window. The glass shattered under the impact, sending shards flying everywhere.

Ethi started to accelerate the car; he left the slum with a rapid speed. Preethi, "Go to my caretaker home, since you were injured heavily." Ethi, "No! It can be done later" in a stubborn tone. Ethi drove the car through the heavy traffic zones at a rapid speed, weaving past cars with inches to spare. Santa dropped his head to Ethi's ear from the back seat and suggested, "Let's do one thing, Ethi! I go to her fiance and extend the task, as you guys were not found in the slum. As soon as possible, send her to the safest place." His face remained calm, and he was unintrested in listening to his voice.

Preethi felt some urge and requested Ethi, "Please! At least stop the vehicle."

Ethi, "Why? No! I can't"

Preethi, with frusturation, asked him, "Will you feed him instead of me?"

Ethi looked puzzled and stopped the car.

Santa left the place to visit her fiance. After Preethi fed her baby inside the car while Ethi stood outside. She bought medical aid such as bandage and ointment and ordered her favorite Badam milk and a tea for Ethi in the nearby teashop. She saw Ethi was sitting on the platform; she went near him and bandaged his wounded elbow and gave him the tea. They both sat together on a platform with their glasses.

Preethi, with a hopeful smile, asked Ethi, "What's your age?"

Ethi, with sipping the tea, replied, "19."

As Preethi's eyes met his eyes, her dimple deepening with a playful smile, she saw him with fondness—not the grown man before her, but a big, fearless child.

Ethi asked about her age; Preethi, with the same smile, replied, "I am 23," and she smiled by turning around.

Ethi asked her strangely, "How do you got yourself to this kind of man?"

Preethi stopped sipping her badam milk, took a heavy breath, and replied, "Huh! I met him when he visited our college as a chief guest to promote his dad's corporate company. Girls in my class had a huge crush over him, even me. We all got attracted to his gestures, charm, and manly voice since he began his speech as 'I am Faisol.' One of my bullies noticed my comments about him and said from my back we should have atleast a good fortune to wish for a man like him. She tested my emotion by triggering my past. As soon as he moved outside, he gave a wink at me, and we shared our contacts. We speak, We speak, huh! Later we got some attachments."
Preethi's face crossed with disappointments and stated, "I thought this was my biggest fortune of my life; later it proved to me today this was the biggest fate of my life."

Later, Ethi finished his tea, and they both noticed a lady who was donating the food parcels for poor people. Preethi pointed to her and stated, "If I had a mom like her, why would I be sitting on these streets?"

Ethi, by holding the tea glass, replied, "She was my mom."

Preethi's eyes froze, unblinking for a minute. Her mind urged him to ask; if she was his mother, why was he sitting with her on the same platform?

There came an old man towards them with her parcel. By pointing her, he stated, "She's a living God, sir." Ethi looked at his mom with his words on his mind. Later, he denied her face and told Preethi to get back to the car. He took her back to his house as he missed something.

V

Draw your own fate

The Ouroboros

Ethi and Preethi finally arrived at the entrance of the slum. Ethi parked the car on the main road. There a traffic police noticed him that his appearance was not even match to the car he parked; he was also shocked by seeing the girl who followed him at the back, and this made him suspect both and he went back to his duty. Ethi secretly brought Preethi to his house. Ethi opened the door silently, and they both entered in. With a haste, Ethi searched for a bag; later he found out that and took 4.8 lakhs from the bag and handed it over to Preethi. Ethi, "Take this money with you and meet my mom's trust in Mumbai by contacting this number; don't worry, I'll be with you and your baby until your departure." Preethi asked him, "How did you get these much money?" Ethi replied to her, "It was given by your fiance as an advance to abort your pregnancy." Preethi stared at him and exclaimed, "Oh!", Preethi asked, "But what I'll be doing there? I didn't even complete my degree." Ethi calmed down her and said, "No worries; say you are a widow; you are there for your baby, and my mom will give you a job like tailoring as well as a room to stay now; take your things from your home." Preethi took all her certificates and some of the stuff from her caretaker home, and she lied to her caretaker that her fiance called her back to Mumbai, where his dad's main branch was located, because she didn't want to break his name or status to her caretaker or anyone. She also informed her that they were going through railways.

Later, Preethi came to Ethi's home and saw a big piano on the side of his room. She asked Ethi with a lot of curiosity, "Do you know to play this?" Ethi, "It belongs to my mom; it was the only thing she left." Preethi asked him, "Not you?" Ethi replied with a hesitation, "Yes!, me too." Preethi, "I can find some deep kind nature in you, man, then why were you doing these silly jobs?"

Ethi accidently pressed a key in the piano; as soon as he pressed, memories opened up.

Ethi, "When I was a kid, Santa seemed to be a hero to me; he was a rugged gangster in my slum, but all says he was a clown on the other side; I saw only the thug side of him. I decided to become like him, but my mom, who was a very spiritual lady, sent me to church and church school to be spiritual like her, but I hate to sing songs in the morning by waking up early. Later I joined hands with Santa; there he gave me a first task by giving me a stone, which was to cut off the street lamp so he could kill the target easily in the moonlight. I did the job well, but he failed, and then he blamed me and prisoned me; hence, he won't get caught up. The founder who came for your delivery was the bishop for the majority of the churches; he was very well known to my mom, so he released me after a hard quarrel with the inspector. And again, church life, I hated to the core. I made an attempt to murder the founder volunteerly in order to go to the cell again. There I met Santa again; he stared at me firmly. Later, he gave some introductions to his known ones, who are all so brutual, they even rape for money. Later, they used me as their informer, surrendering for the cases that were done by them or Santa. Days passed, and I accombined with Santa and became involved in many child kidnaps, money threats, tender threats, land threats, etc. It was my fate to have the venom at my neck and to have some political influences through him. When I got released after the attempted murder case, I saw my mom was swifting from her home; she took all her things as a load in order to shift to a new area; hence, this locality was so violent. My mom asked for a last time, "If you don't come with me, I'll tell the truck driver to take the truck." As a 10-year-old boy struggling to hold back tears, I replied, "Okay!, you go," and she was gone. I was crying under the piano after her absence; this piano was the only thing she left as it was too heavy to carry. I sat under this piano, and my mom will

sing some spiritual songs, and I see her wonderment from down. hah!" Ethi laughed with pain.

Preethi felt sad for Ethi, and she realized there was no time to help him by seeing her watch. Then Ethi and Preethi were ready to move to the railways. There Kundhavali saw their departure from the home; she took her phone silently and informed Vincent of this.

Vincent suddenly rang to Faisol and informed him, "Man, she was moving with the boy to the railways with her baby." Faisol with a big relief, "Ha! Let her leave; I think she won't make this sensitive." Vincent alerted Faisol, "Man, she mentioned she was going to Mumbai; what if she goes to your dad's company over there and he is there now?" Faisol was back to his same old mood and exclaimed, "Oh! Why does this shit always happen to me? Yes! She was the person to do that too. Vincent, I am totally dumb now. Please do something."

Vincent found his next move and replied, "Okay! I'll handle it" and cuts the call.

VI

Fate joins their journey

Labyrinth

As Ethi and Preethi reached the main road, the traffic police over there noticed that car again. Ethi stopped the car as it was jamed. The traffic police asked an old constable nearby about Ethi by pointing towards his face in the car window, and the old constable replied, "Yes, sir, these guys are very dangerous; they involved in many child kidnaps, street fights, chain snatchings, smuggling, even some rapes, and also..." The traffic police said, "Ok! Stop your list; I already had a doubt over his costly car, which didn't even match his appearance." The old constable said, "May be some car theft." The traffic policeman stated, "But I had also noticed a girl with him." The old constable noticed that girl in the car and said, "Yes!, sir," in a base tone. The traffic police said, "Stop! The car; after all, vehicles yet to go."

The old constable stopped Ethi's car and asked, "Hm! car's book?" Ethi couldn't find out anything; hence, it was not his car; it was used by the goons of her fiance. The traffic police declared, "Hence it's a suspect of prostitution; you both come outside." Preethi reacted suddenly and stated, "What? Sir, he is a friend of mine," he replied, "Is he? You seem so elite; see his face; does it have any match?" Ethi was dumb; he didn't know what to do, and they both were taken inside the station.

The traffic policeman commanded, "Constable, take him to your custody." The traffic policeman got a view of her dark saree, which exposed some skin of her, and he slowly went near her. Preethi felt uneasy as the traffic police officer's gaze lingered on her. She adjusted her saree, sensing his intrustive stare.

The traffic policeman asked, "Are there any lady cops over here?"
All the lady cops over there minded their own business; all pretended that they didn't listen to him.

By noticing all this, the old constable said, "No, sir," and bowed his head down.

The traffic policeman said, "Then I should treat you, little lady, oh, sorry! Little Mummy!" and slowly rubbed her arms. Preethi analyzed his touches with the wrong intention and pushed his hands away.

The traffic policeman exclaimed, "Ah! This was the biggest mistake than you did in the car. If you adjuse me here, I'll leave you alone."

Preethi looked for Ethi. Ethi was hold by the cops firmly, and the old constable gestured for the cops to release their hands by believing that he could do something to save the two innocent children. And they can't do it so.

The traffic policeman man analyzed her thoughts in his way and offered her, "Okay! Take your friend with you; now satisfy me and take him for your satisfaction whenever you want."

Preethi felt awkward; the traffic policeman hugged her harshly, and suddenly her baby started crying. Preethi pushed him, but she couldn't, as she was not physically matched to him.

All the lady cops and aged cops over there turned their heads; hence, they can't see this scene.

The traffic policeman closed the baby's mouth and put his face towards Preethi's hair to smell the scent of her hair. The entire station fell silent, with only the man's labored breathing audible as he leaned in, inhaling the scent of her hair.

Just then, the Ratchasan party leader, Ratchasan, burst into the station, flinging open the doors and disrupting the tense scene. Accompanied by press members, he began recording the incident, seeking to capitalize on the situation and garner public support for the distressed lady.

Ratchasan asked his party member, "How was my performance?"

He exclaimed, "Huge one, thalaivare!"

Ratchasan stated to the traffic policeman, "This record is enough to put you in the cell and also for my votes," and asked his PA, "Am I correct?"

He exclaimed, "Yes! Boss, you are the hero of this city from today, boss," and chanted, "Long live! Ratchasan," and all the members over there chanted the same.

Ethi and Preethi silently moved from there, and he noticed Ethi and called him, "Hey! Santa's Boy, did he trouble you so much? Don't worry, I send this to media by giving them dvds, haha!"

The traffic policeman felt that he was caught in the rat trap with a fraction of a second.

Ratchasan, "Oh! It seems like you are in love and you guys are so fast," and he noticed their luggage in their hands and asked them, "Are you going somewhere to start a new life? Take this money with you" and advised Preethi, "And you, don't wait for a person like me to save you always."

Ethi and Preethi got into their car with the baby. Ethi felt some relief that finally he got some big influence. While driving, Preethi murmered, "Yes, all men are same in nature."

Ethi asked, "What? but why?"

Preethi, "No need of arguments, since this is my personal issue, I have faced since my childhood." Ethi smiled sarcastically and continued driving.

Then they reached railways and walked among crowds; suddenly, an unknown hand among the crowd pulled the baby out of his hand. With warp speed, Ethi choked his neck from the back, and Preethi took her baby back. Then the man used a sharp knife to escape from Ethi's choke and moved away from him. When he moved, a group of Chinese goons joined. As this departure planned was leaked from her caretaker to Vincent. Ethi warned Preethi to go to the opposite platform before he warned she went. Ethi fought the group of men in the crowd and tried to escape from them; hence, they had heavy thug tools.

Ethi tried to go to the opposite platform where Preethi stood with her baby; he headed towards her, but unfortunately a man from there had thrown the Chinese blade to his injured knee. Seizing the opportunity, the men charged towards him, but their move was paused by a passing train. Preethi, witnessing the chaos, cried out in distress, "Ethi, Ethi!" by noticing the moving train, towards Ethi, She hastily set her baby down and rushed towards him. As she rushed, she lost her foot on the loose stones; she slipped and fell down. The train was a little far to them with ear-splitting horns. She quickly regained her balance, spirited towards Ethi, and pushed him safely onto her platform. The train roared by, mere feet away. Startled by the deafening sound, her baby burst into tears. Preethi and Ethi escaped from them.

Preethi asked him, "Are you okay, Ethi?" in a caring manner, and she gave him water from the car.

Ethi drank it, and while he was drinking, he burst out of laughter by spitting out the water.

Preethi was shocked by his sudden behavior and asked him, "Are you mad?"

Ethi asked, "Why did you save this man?who has the same nature as you mentioned earlier."

Ethi stopped his laughter and told her to get in. Preethi's face was left unanswerable for his question.

Later, they decided to go to the airport; hence, this station was surrounded by them. They reached the airport, and there Ethi noticed the same goons over there. Preethi's face is drowned to tense by the question; Why does he want to kill her baby? Preethi finally decided and said Ethi, "Lets move up to him; why should I fear over him and run here and there since I didn't make any mistake than loving a man like him?"

Ethi remained calm, and with a heavy breath, he got inside the car by gesturing for her to get in.

VII

Preethi! find the answer for your fates

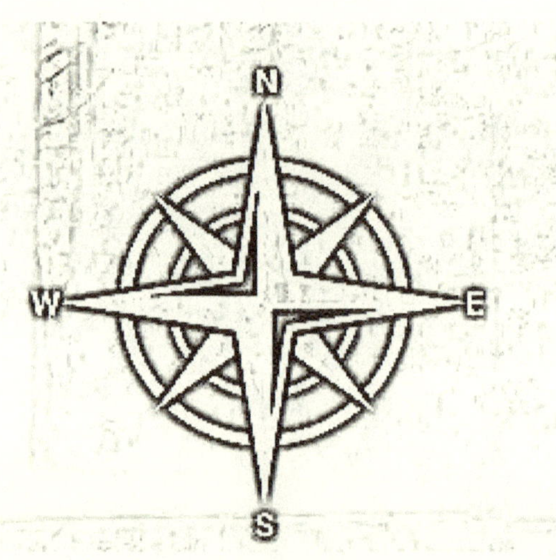

Compass.

They reached his dad's company, and when Ethi came out of his car, he noticed the building, which was so tall and big. There Santa arrived and welcomed them and said, "All are alright; you go and talk to his father first." Preethi said,

"Ethi it's personal, so let me go alone." Ethi accepted her wish, and he stepped backward to sit in the car. Preethi went to the third floor where her fiance dad Ammar welcomed her and said, "I came to know everything by his PA Vincent; he told everything after I saw the news which telecast the harassment happened to you in the police station, and I found out our company logo in the car, then I asked him. See, I am straightforward. I know you love my son because of our status; unfortunately, he can't be with you since he got many debts from his uncle, and Faisol's uncle pressured him to marry off his daughter, seeking to control half of Faisol's inheritance through the strategic union. Why do you want to suffer at this age by holding a baby in your arms, child? As you loved my son, I guarantee a secure future and educational support for you, as I am aware of your circumstances through Faisol's PA, so give your baby to me. I will take care of it as my child. Once Faisol settles in Mumbai with his wife and uncle to manage the main branch, I'll be left alone."

Preethi fell for his words and handed over the baby to him. Ammar took the baby in his hands and steered milk by mixing some powder. Ethi noticed this from down through the glass of the window. Ethi, "Santa, see there, once you kidnapped the kids, you used that powder for making them unconscious, right? But you'll do that for kids above 6 or 10; the child who went inside was just 3 weeks old." Santa was in a confused state and replied, "Yes! Ethi."

Ethi suddenly ran to the entrance, followed by Santa. Santa stopped Ethi by placing his hands firmly on his shoulder and said, "You have a different and huge task to do here." Ethi felt something strange was near; suddenly Santa pushed Ethi towards the opened elevator, and he was grabbed by two Chinese goons as the elevator doors closed. Ethi witnessed a shocking betrayal etched on Santa's face, leaving him stunned. They brought Ethi to the half-constructed underground floor. He was tied up by ropes on the chair and heavily beat by Chinese. A man over there mocked his young appearance and said, "Ó! Tā shì nàgè rén ma? Chéng lǐ hǎoxiàng méiyǒu chéngnián de bàotú" and all laughed harder. Ethi stayed calm and tried to think smarter; he figured out the surroundings for some things to defend them, but there was only a fire extinguisher little behind him.

On the other side, Preethi thoughts seesawed with joy and worry as she gazed at her baby.

Meanwhile, Ethi felt he was racing against time. The Chinese man slapped Ethi's head. Ethi bowed down his head, and he found out a big nail, where its head emerged out of the broken chair, he seated and made his job easier. With a rapid force, Ethi stamped the nail's head down towards the foot of the Chinese man. Chinese man screamed in agony, "Ahw!" He triggered his pistol accidentally to the fire extinguisher by the agony; it burst out and the place filled with carbon dioxide. Ethi took advantage; he spotted a gas-wielding machine as the floor filled with Co2, its flame flickering due to Co2 pressure. With swift action, Ethi jumped sideways with the chair and used that flame to untie his hands. He took off his knife and choked the Chinese man towards the wall and threatened him to call Faisol to know where he was. He asked him, "Say him to come to this floor," and he did as well as he said. Then Ethi entered the elevator.

Faisol was seeing his mobile without noticing Ethi's presence while entering the elevator. Ethi emerged from the front corner of the door and locked Faisol with his knife. Since Ethi caught him by hiding in the corner, they can't face each other. Faisol face crossed with tremendous shock and asked him, "Hey! Who is this?" Ethi, "The man, oops! sorry! The boy you have asked for," Faisol, "Don't overact; just be in your role." Ethi threatened him, "I believe you're well informed; before she departs for Mumbai, I'll depart your body to your dad when the 3rd floor comes."

And the elevator reached the 3rd floor. Ethi warned Preethi, "Preethi! Get in soon; take the child from him; don't believe *him; he is more dangerous than his son." Ammar, "Hey! Who is this kid, Vincent? She is our girl, boy." Ethi remained dumb.*

As Preethi too remained calm, her child pulled her chain, his eyes wide with fear, and started crying, silently begging, 'Don't leave me behind, please! take me home' Preethi suddenly took her child from Ammar; Ammar got a little jerk. Preethi exclaimed, "Oh! Your girl, Ethi, hold him for a second. I want to ensure something for them. It won't take much time to act like you guys; I proved it until you signed the check, and you think I am a human trafficker? or fraud like your son and you?" Faisol suddenly raised his voice and said, "Hey! whether your father is a gentleman? Daughter of a pervert bastard, you don't have any rights to talk about my dad."

Preethi replied suddenly, "But I am not like him, but you're father like son. If I am just Preethi, I might believe your words and accept all your deals. But now I am mom of my own child. Just a minute right! to change any individuals with the smells of unearned money, but my son saved me from that minute. I don't want your check; have it with you. I can grow him up without the smells of unearned money and mark it! One day, he'll be the boss of you guys. Ethi! Let's move."

And Ethi pushed Faisol towards the door. Preethi and Faisol stared at each other firmly. Preethi got into the elevator with her baby. As the doors closed, Preethi stated, "I won't make any sensitive content to media about your son using my child as a witness; don't worry about it; get your son married to that rich woman."

Ammar felt humilated by Preethi's words in his company; all his night shift employers saw that scene, which made Ammar get humilated more. With that humilation, he slapped his son and said annoyingly, "If you can't make it right, just quit from it." He went near the window and commanded the Chinese goons to terminate them. Ammar by pointing Santa and ordered them, "Get that bald man too, who played double game with us." Santa rushed to the Ethi's car door. Ethi refused to open the door and said, "Still, I don't want to wrap the same serpent around my neck; you can only spit venoms, Santa. It's time to cut it off. Anyway, you're good in alternative ways, so we can meet if you're alive after I drop her." and he made Santa distressed and took the car; the Chinese goons sliced Santa into pieces and chased the car.

VIII

Fate: But I have an other idea

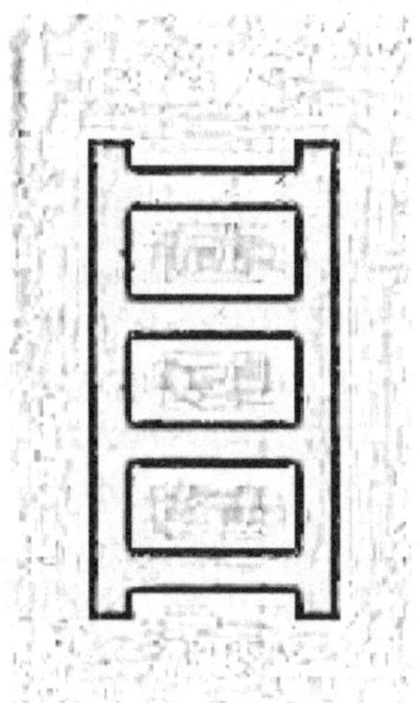

The Owuo Atwedee

As Ethi drove the car from Ammar's company, he suddenly got jammed in traffic. Ethi noticed at the backside; he didn't find out any goons. But the Chinese group had found out they were far away in the jam. After the jam cleared, horns echoed through the air; they followed silently, Ethi and Preethi. They took a Molotav cocktail in their hands, and after they followed them on the silent highway, they accelerated their car with a rapid speed. Preethi asked Ethi, "Where are you going now?" Ethi was totally exhausted and replied, "Harbour." Preethi turned her head silently. Suddenly, the Chinese gang crossed their way and tossed the molotav cocktail in the tires; the back tires of the car are blazing with fire. Suddenly, Ethi swiftly steered his car to the seashore, and the sand effectively smothered the flames, extinguishing the fire. The vehicle stopped running because it had run out of fuel.

Ethi was stressed out; loosened his grip on the steering wheel. Ethi opened the doors of the car and warned Preethi, "Don't come out until I say." Suddenly, a song played in the car FM with the lyrics; 'Yedhaiyum thaangum idhayam irundhaal, irudhi varaikum amaidhi irukum.' Ethi tried to stop it, Preethi catched his hands and said, "It's my favorite song; let me listen." Then Ethi heroically came out of the car and stood tall, his silhouette illuminated by the soft, silvery moonlight. Before him, a semicircle of over ten men formed a menacing arc, their faces shrouded in shadows. They can hear only the sounds of the melody drifting from the car's stereo and the sounds of heavy wind at night. The smell of salty sea filled their nostrils. Ethi asked heroically, "Bro, you asked for a gangster? Welcome to the city of thugs."

With a swift motion, all stepped their foots in the shore and marched towards Ethi. Ethi used his street fight techniques to defend their martial arts. Ethi was exhausted to the core and breathed heavily. Seizing this opportunity, the men formed a semicircle again, took out their sharp Chinese blades, and rapidly scratched Ethi. His chest and abdomen flesh were torn out, and he was flooding in blood. He slowly dragged his body towards the car trunk, placing his hand there for support. He slowly moved his hands towards his belt and lossened it; all the men's eyes were stranged by his action, an eagle on the boat looked at him firmly by slowly swaying its head from left to right; all the men were stunned by his action, He hold a thing firmly, which was between his belt; he suprisingly took his sentimental knife, Ethi hand closed around his sentimental knife as the men approached. Exhaustion seemed to overcome him and he sank to the ground, the blade stood firmly in the sand. But his eyes told a diffrent story-sharp, and piercing than the knife. The eagle let out a haunting cry and took to the skies, spreaded its wings, as it was in the tight spot.

All men grabbed their blades firmly. In the blink of an eye, a man from his side moved towards him. Ethi pierced his foot with his knife and rapidly pierced his feet. One more man marched towards him with his heavy blade; Ethi slid in sands and cut off his nerves in the backfoot. With a swift motion, Ethi caught the neck of a man and choked it, hold his knife firmly until his palm got red, and brutually inserted his knife to his shoulders. He left the grip of the knife after that; he was bleeding to the core and moved towards them; he noticed only 4 men left. The eyes of the men only saw the vampire towards them instead of Ethi. One man stepped slowly towards him and threatened him with his blade. With a lightening speed, Ethi pierced his eyes using the fingers; his fingers jerked down to the core, and he took his bloody hands from the collapsed eyes. Ethi's fingers were wet with the eye fluids. The remaining men were done with his action, and they stepped backward, threw the molotav cocktail in the car, and ran away.

Preethi took her baby and ran out of the blazzing car. Preethi spotted a group of men in the distance and sensed danger looming and sprang into action, dashing towards Ethi. Ethi noticed her frantic spirit, and without sensing anything, he ran back towards her. He swiftly crossed in front of her with a decisive gesture; he beckoned her to follow him towards the ship. He sprinted towards the ship, his feet pounding the sand in a desperate bid for escape. But fate had other plans. As he was a little far from the ship, an anchor hung at the tip of a ship swung ominously in the moonlight. Ethi momentum carried him forward, and he collided with the rusty metal. The anchor's curved edge sliced across his neck, his body crumpled to the shore. Blood spilled from his neck, forming a dark, glossy pool that reflected the moon's pale light. His eyes locked onto the moon above, fading to black. Each breathe is weaker than the last, and his breath has stopped.

Ethi had his last breath

Preethi's face widened with tremendous sorrowfulness; she was confused for her next move since the goons were near. She immediately hid herself in between the ship and placed her baby in the box, which contained old newspapers. Suddenly, she was spotted by the goons when she dropped down from the ship. Seeking an escape, as she marched towards the highways, a goon hurled an axe through the air. It stuck her back, biting deep into her flesh. Preethi screamed; her last breath flew like a bird set free, when she fell down on the shore, stirring the sand beside her.

The goons rang Ammar and informed him, "All are done. Only the child was missing."
Ammar ordered, "Okay! Leave the child; he doesn't know what's going on; dispose of their bodies in the sea and come back."

Later, the ship begun to move, a box fell down to the floor, and there Preethi's baby burst out of crying, and it was noticed by a prostitute lady. She handed over the little one to her boss. Her boss tossed peanuts into her mouth and replied, "What can we do with this boy child? It won't help in our business; throw it away." Later, the lady noticed a man with a long white dress, and it was none other than the founder. She pointed out that man ordered her, "Go and give to the man who was covered with white and ask some amount; he seems like he would take it." The prostitute lady went near him and asked, "Can you take this child with you?" The founder saw her firmly; later he replied, "Sure! give it ", The prostitute lady demanded the amount of Rs. 200, and the founder turned his head with disappointment and replied, "Oh! then have it with you." Later, she told him what her boss lady had said when she saw this baby. Later, the founder accepted the deal and got the baby. A sudden raid happened on the ship by navy officers; they spotted prostitutes over there and the lady who was holding the 200 rupees. One navyman got those 200 rupees and chased them away.,

IX
The Wheel of karma

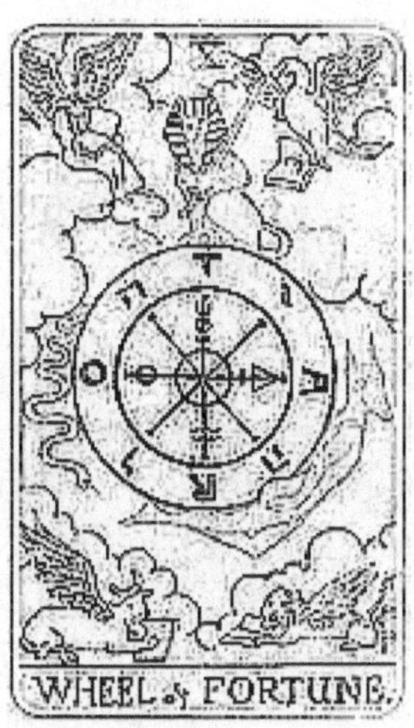

The wheel of fortune

After a six-year span, Preethi's child grew up in the founder orphanage in Mumbai. The growing child worked for others secretly in the orphanage for money to buy some snacks, as he hated trust foods. One fresh day, the child was sitting on the floor and noticed that all other kids were adopted except him. There arrived the old philosopher and sat near him. He then noticed the child was holding a chocolate; he ordered him, "Give that chocolate to me." The child gestured no and gestured his five fingers to show him the cost. He was shocked by his gesture and asked him, "Where did you get this?" The child gestured by using his hand to show that shop, which was outside. He asked again, "Did they give it for free?" The child gestured no. The philosopher laughed and exclaimed, "Wow! You have decided to eat on your own money at this age." Later, he noticed the child was seeing the couples who were visiting the orphanage. The philosopher started his advice, "See my child, you're lucky to be here. Why are you nagging for a couple's love? when we are children of God, like Jesus. Todays parents have time to earn money more than spending time with their children; still, you need them?" The child looked into his eyes through blurred tears with lots of innocence.

On the other side, far across the city, Faisol was crying by seeing the wallet that contained Preethi's photo. He was far beside the memorable frame of Ammar and asked his apology to his gone girl friend; though he wanted to abort her pregnancy because of the family pressure, he still had feelings for her. There his wife entered the room. Faisol wiped out his tears and welcomed her, "Come inside, Ms. Gold Digger." She asked him, "Why do you call me like that, honey? You just prick me always," in a distressed tone. Faisol burst out of anger and explained to her, "How to call you then? My fate: I got money for my debt from your dad since I thought he was a gentleman, but he twisted that as marriage threatens for marrying an infertile woman like you."

She said, "Oh! then thats a problem, right?" in an innocent tone.

He shouted by closing the door and said to her, "Yes! If I don't get an heir, your father will take advantage, and he will grab everything from me; he is a man to do that." His wife's distress was triggered again by the harsh sound of the slammed door.

Meanwhile, the child was stressed out of the philosopher's advice. There came a man with his wife to the orphanage, who was covered with costly attire. He went to the reception, and the receptionist saw his face, which was very familiar to her, and asked him, "Sir, I've seen you in ads and on big flexes," and then she looked down, her mind reeling. He cracked a laugh and replied to her, "I am the manager of Techspark Pvt. Ltd., Faisol." The receptionist exclaimed, "Whoa! Finally, I can remember. Did you come for the adoption?" Faisol's face remained calm and unintrested of her question; hence, he came for the sake of his wife. Her wife saw many beautiful faces was running across the hall; one face attracted her more. She gestured for the Preethi's child to come to her; thus, she loved his face. She said to her husband, "I like his gratitude at this age; he just ran towards us when I called him; let's adopt him." Then the founder arrived there; she went towards him with Preethi's child and asked him, "Is he a mute boy? He seems too old to speak." The founder replied, "He speaks rarely; he always remains alone." Her face flooded with pittyness and she exclaimed, "Oh!" and asked for his name.

The founder got some nervous since he took him from the ship. Later he replied with a relaxation, "Ethi," as this name was very familiar to him. Faisol smiled at him, and the child smiled back. Faisol saw the child face and murmured, "Your dimple reminds me of something."

And they both took him home by filling out the procedure form. Preethi's child waved his hand with a smile as bye to the philosopher. The philosopher murmured his last advice, "Fates of life are unpredictable, but karma will rewrite it any day."

THE END

Preethi's child with his new mom

Hi! I am your Abishek.J, hope all you enjoyed my first novel. If you like it, please share to your friends and family. Give your feedbacks, comments and reviews in amazon or notion press. Further details, contact: 8438865233, insta: @abireigns and facebook: abireigns.

THANK YOU!

www.ingramcontent.com/pod-product-compliance
Lightning Source LLC
LaVergne TN
LVHW040949150826
845672LV00002B/614

* 9 7 9 8 8 9 5 8 8 1 9 1 0 *